Secret
PRINCESSES

D0434482

Special thanks to Linda Chapman

For Klara Strange, who has a big smile and an even bigger love of magic!

ORCHARD BOOKS

First published in Great Britain in 2017 by The Watts Publishing Group

1 3 5 7 9 10 8 6 4 2

A CIP catalogue record for this book
is available from the British Library.

ISBN 978 1 40833 616 8

Printed and bound in Great Britain by Clays Ltd, St Ives plc

The paper and board used in this book are made from wood from responsible sources.

Orchard Books
An imprint of
Hachette Children's Group
Part of The Watts Publishing Group Limited
Carmelite House
50 Victoria Embankment
London EC4Y 0DZ

An Hachette UK Company
www.hachette.co.uk
www.hachettechildrens.co.uk

Series created by Hothouse Fiction
www.hothousefiction.com

Puppy Magic

ROSIE BANKS

Wishing Star Palace

The Secret Princess Promise

"I promise that I will be kind and brave,
Using my magic to help and save,
Granting wishes and doing my best,
To make people smile and bring happiness."

CONTENTS

CHAPTER ONE

The Magic Begins!

"One … two … three …" Charlotte Williams counted the seconds as she stood in a perfect handstand, her toes pointing up towards the bright blue sky. The short, dry grass was warm under her fingers and she could smell the sweet oranges ripening on the trees in the back yard. Her brown curls brushed the ground. "Four … five … six …"

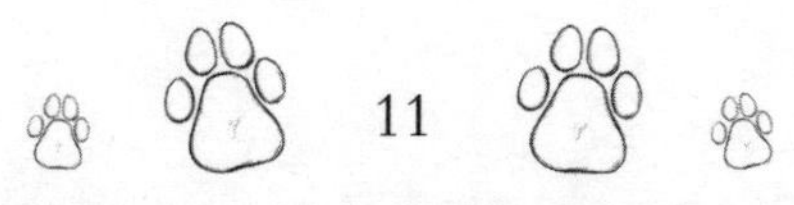

"Charlotte!" Mrs Williams opened the back door. "I'm just talking to Mia's mum on the computer. Do you want to have a chat with Mia?"

"Of course!" Charlotte's feet touched the grass. Leaping up, she ran over to her mum. "It's ages since I spoke to her!"

Mrs Williams's eyes twinkled. "You mean three whole days."

Charlotte grinned. "That's ages for me and Mia!" She and Mia were best friends. They used to live in the same village in England, until Charlotte's family had moved to California. Although Charlotte had made lots of new friends in America, no one would ever replace Mia.

She hurried inside to the study. The air conditioning was on, keeping the house lovely and cool. When Charlotte had first moved to California she'd found it strange being able to wear shorts every day.

Mia was on the computer screen. Her long, blonde hair was tucked behind her ears and she was wearing her pyjamas and her dressing gown. Seeing Charlotte, she waved. "Hi!"

Happiness fizzed through Charlotte as she sat down.

"Hi!" she said. "What have you been up to?"

"Just normal weekend stuff," said Mia. "We went for a bike ride this morning and then I went to see my Auntie Marie and helped take her dogs for a walk. How about you?"

"I went to a baseball game with Liam and Harvey," said Charlotte.

Just then, a little girl with blonde hair in bunches popped her head over Mia's shoulder. It was Elsie, Mia's younger sister. "Hello, Charlotte! Guess what? I can ride my bike without stabilisers now."

"Wow! Well done, Elsie," said Charlotte.

"Are Mia and Elsie there?" Liam and Harvey, Charlotte's six-year-old twin brothers, came barrelling into the study.

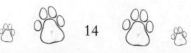

"Hi, Mia! Hi, Elsie!" they shouted.

"Look, we lost our front teeth!" said Liam, opening his mouth in front of the computer's camera to show them that one of his front teeth had fallen out.

"You've got matching gaps!" said Mia.

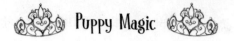

"Come on, boys," Mrs Williams said, coming into the room. "Leave Charlotte and Mia to have a chat. It might be lunchtime here, but it's evening in England and Mia will probably have to go to bed soon."

Mia waved goodbye to the twins and then persuaded Elsie to go and play. Finally, she and Charlotte were able to chat uninterrupted. They caught up about school and everything else they'd been doing until Mia's mum broke into the conversation. "Time to say goodbye and go to bed, Mia!" she called. "You can chat again soon."

Charlotte touched the half-heart pendant she wore around her neck. "Hopefully very soon," she said, winking at Mia.

Mia held up her own matching pendant and grinned happily. "Oh, yes," she said, winking back.

Charlotte felt a warm glow in her tummy.

She and Mia shared the most amazing secret. When she had moved to America, their old babysitter, Alice, had given them both magic necklaces!

Whenever the necklaces started to glow, Mia and Charlotte were whisked away to an incredibly beautiful palace high up in the clouds. The first time Charlotte and Mia had arrived at Wishing Star Palace, Alice had explained that they'd been chosen to train as Secret Princesses – special girls who used magic to make wishes come true! Charlotte loved everything about training to be a Secret Princess. It meant she got to help people, do magic – and best of all, have adventures with Mia!

Gazing at the pendant in her hand, Charlotte thought longingly, *Oh, I wish we could go to Wishing Star Palace now.* On their last adventure, she and Mia had passed the first stage of their training and earned gorgeous diamond tiaras that they could wear whenever they visited the palace. Now, for the second stage of their training, they needed to help four more people. If they did, they'd earn sparkling ruby princess slippers that would let them travel by magic. It was all so exciting!

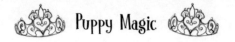

Charlotte saw light flicker across the surface of her pendant. She caught her breath and peered closer. Was she imagining it? No – the pendant was starting to glow!

Charlotte looked at Mia, who was staring at her own necklace. It was glowing too! The girls grinned at each other, then Charlotte shut down the computer and ran to her bedroom, her heart racing. No time would pass while she was away, but she still didn't want her family to see her magically vanish! Shutting the door behind her, she opened her fingers. The magic pendant was now glowing like a ray of sunshine.

"I wish I could see Mia at Wishing Star Palace!" Charlotte whispered.

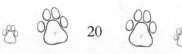

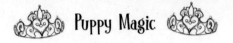

Light blazed out, surrounding her. She felt it swirl around and lift her up and away. Excitement flashed through Charlotte. Another magical Secret Princess adventure was about to begin!

CHAPTER TWO

Amazing Animals

Charlotte's feet came to rest on velvety soft grass. She opened her eyes and saw that she was standing in front of Wishing Star Palace. Flags flew from its four turrets, ivy climbed up its marble walls, and its heart-shaped windows glinted in the sunlight.

"Yay!" cried Charlotte, twirling on the spot. The long, pink princess dress she'd

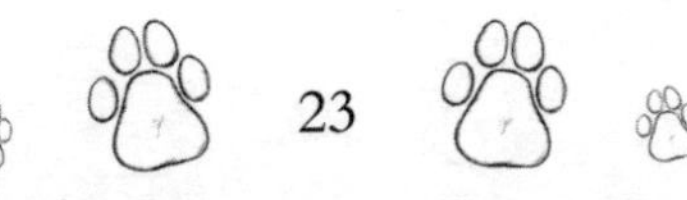

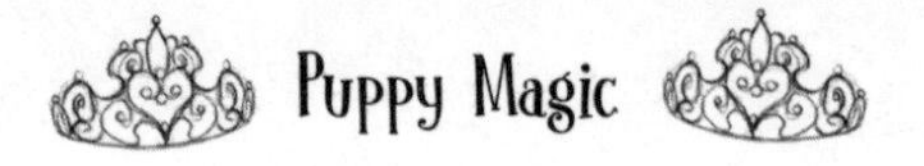

magically changed into swished around her legs. Putting a hand up to her head, she smiled as she felt her diamond tiara resting on her brown curls.

"Charlotte!" Mia peeked out from behind a nearby tree with pink candyfloss and candy canes hanging from its branches. She was wearing a beautiful golden dress with silver embroidery and her own diamond tiara nestled in her blonde hair.

They ran to meet each other and hugged.

"It's so brilliant to see you," said Mia. "I mean, it's great talking on the computer but it's even better to be together for real!"

Charlotte knew just what she meant. She was so happy she felt like turning a cartwheel but she knew it might be tricky in her dress. "And the palace looks great!" she said, looking at the glittering turrets.

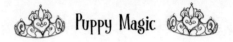

When they had first come to Wishing Star Palace, it had looked very different. Princess Poison, a Secret Princess who had turned bad, had put a spell on the palace. With every wish she ruined, she'd made the palace crumble and break. But by granting four people's wishes, Mia and Charlotte had helped mend the palace, and earned their princess tiaras.

"It looks so much better," agreed Mia. She looked towards the doorway. "Should we see if anyone is inside?"

Wishing Star Palace was where all the Secret Princesses stayed when they were using magic to help people with their wishes, but they each had jobs in the real world, too.

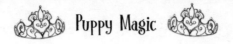

One of the princesses was a baker, another was an artist, and Alice, who had given them their necklaces, was a pop star! Each princess had her own special talent, but they were all kind and fun.

Mia tucked her hand through Charlotte's arm and they started walking towards the palace. As they got closer, five birds came round the side of the palace. They had long multicoloured tails trailing behind them and looked like big, golden peacocks.

Suddenly, all the birds lifted their tails and opened them at the same time. Mia and Charlotte gasped in delight. The birds' tails had layers of bright feathers in all the colours of the rainbow!

The birds bobbed their golden heads at the girls. They walked over and started nuzzling them with their beaks.

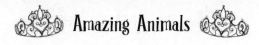

"You're very friendly!" said Mia, laughing.

"Our Rainbow Birds seem to like you!" called a voice.

Mia and Charlotte saw Alice coming out of Wishing Star Palace with Princess Ella and another princess they didn't recognise.

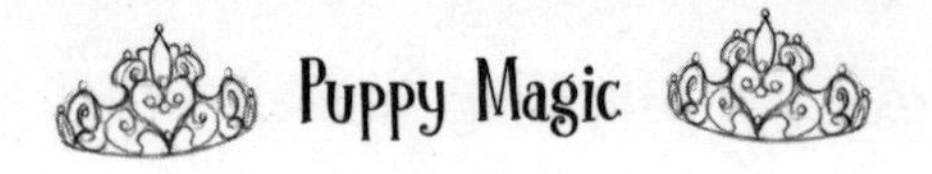

She had short curly hair, a trendy striped dress, and a pendant shaped like a thimble.

"Girls, I don't think you've met Princess Cara before," Alice said. "She's a fashion designer in the real world. She designed the costumes for my last tour."

"It's lovely to meet you both. I've heard lots about you. How are you?" Cara said, tucking some strands of her brown hair behind her ears as she hurried over.

"Really good – especially now we're here," said Charlotte, grinning at her best friend.

"I really like your dress," Mia said.

"Thanks!" said Princess Cara with a big smile. "Your dresses are pretty, too!"

"Is there someone in the Magic Mirror who needs our help, Alice?" Mia added, eagerly.

"Not right now," said Alice, with a smile. "But hopefully soon. You need to grant four wishes and earn four rubies to get your princess slippers." She pulled up the bottom of her dress and showed the girls her glittery ruby shoes.

Charlotte and Mia grinned at each other in delight.

"But for now, Ella wanted you to visit because she needs a hand with the animals," Alice explained.

"I really do," said Princess Ella. "There are so many wonderful creatures here at Wishing Star Palace and I love looking after them all, but they can be a handful – like these Rainbow Birds. They keep escaping into the garden." One of the birds nudged her with its beak until she stroked his head. She giggled. "You are very naughty," she told it. "You know you're not supposed to wander this far from the pond. I suppose you were after the candyfloss, as usual?"

The bird quickly shook its head but Princess Ella plucked a strand of pink candyfloss from its feathers. "Hmm," she said, raising her dark eyebrows. "I think it's high time we get you back to your nests before you

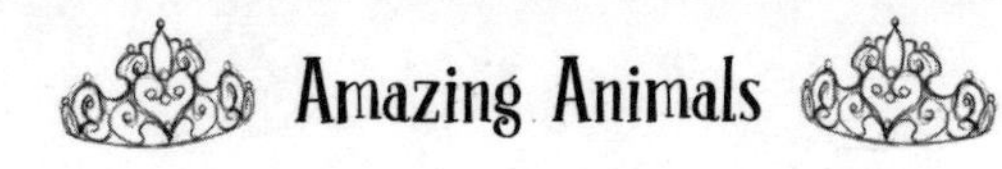

give yourselves tummy aches." She glanced at Mia and Charlotte. "Will you girls help?"

"Oh, yes!" they said.

"Would you mind if I stayed here?" said Alice. "I'm working on a song for my next album and I really want to go to the music room and finish it."

"And I was planning to take a walk around the gardens – I need inspiration for my next collection," said Princess Cara.

"That's fine," Princess Ella told them.

"Don't worry," said Mia. "We would love to help."

Alice said goodbye and hurried off.

Charlotte turned to Princess Ella. "How do we get the birds back to their nests?"

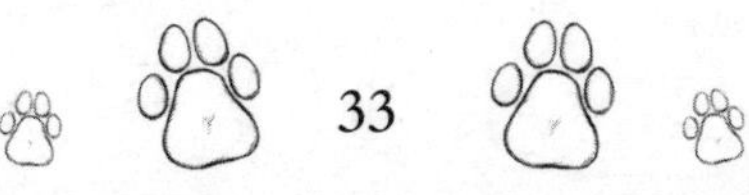

"We'll use my special jeep," said Princess Ella. "It's just around the corner." She led the way round the side of the palace to where a silver jeep was parked with its top down. Its paint sparkled in the sun and it had purple velvet seats and a glittering steering wheel.

"Awesome!' said Charlotte, running over to the car. "I love it."

Ella grinned. “Me too. I wish I could drive it back home, but it’s so shiny it might scare the horses and cows when I go on my visits!” In the real world Ella was a vet. “Anyway, hop in!”

The girls jumped into the back and pulled the door shut. Princess Ella got into the front and grinned at them over her shoulder.

"Are you ready for some fun?" she asked.

"Yes!" they cried.

Princess Ella's brown eyes sparkled. She tapped the steering wheel three times with her wand. "Then fasten your seat belts – it's time to fly!"

CHAPTER THREE
An Unwelcome Visitor

Both girls squealed as white, feathered wings shot out of the jeep's sides. The wings flapped up and down and the jeep took off into the blue sky!

Princess Ella giggled as she saw the girls' stunned faces. "I told you it was special!"

Charlotte and Mia looked out over the sides as the magical jeep flew up into the air.

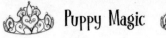

They glided around Wishing Star Palace to where the Rainbow Birds were pecking at the grass with their beaks. "Here," said Ella, passing them some bags of glittering seed from the seat next to her. "Scatter some of these seeds so the birds will follow us."

"But won't the seeds fall on the ground?" said Mia, sounding puzzled.

"Try it," urged Ella.

The girls threw out handfuls of seeds. The seeds fell in a sparkling stream, not falling but trailing in the air like ribbons. The birds looked up and squawked eagerly, flying up to peck at the trails of seeds. They followed the jeep, gobbling up the seeds as Charlotte and Mia threw more and more handfuls.

“I’ll fly us back to the pond where the birds live,” said Ella. She steered the jeep higher into the sky and, with the birds flying after them, they soared over the gorgeous turrets of the palace.

“Look at that swimming pool!” cried Charlotte, pointing out a blue pool down below with diving boards and twisty pink and purple water slides.

"And those trampolines!" said Mia, noticing ten different trampolines of all shapes and sizes. A princess with straight, dark hair was bouncing on them and doing flips in the air. Ella honked the jeep's horn. The princess looked up and waved as the girls and the birds flew past.

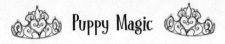

"That's Princess Kiko," Ella said. "She's a champion gymnast back in the real world."

"Wow!" said Charlotte. "I can't wait to meet her." Charlotte loved gymnastics, too.

They glided over a maze made with neat green hedges, then past a garden filled with beautiful marble statues of princesses, a meadow, a tennis court and a carousel with painted horses.

"I never knew there was so much to see in the gardens," said Charlotte.

"Is that the pond?" said Mia, pointing to an enormous blue pond edged with palm trees. In the middle of the pond, fountains sprayed water into the air.

"That's it!" said Ella cheerfully. "It's one

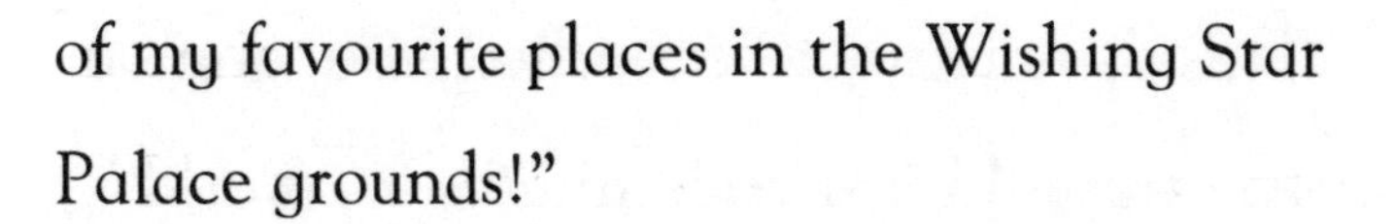

of my favourite places in the Wishing Star Palace grounds!"

As Ella headed the jeep down to land, the girls noticed flamingo-like birds standing in the pond, their feathers changing colour every few seconds from neon pink to bright yellow and then fluorescent green. Turtles were swimming lazily in the water, their shells shining with diamonds. A herd of unicorns with long, silky manes were drinking at the edge of the pond, their horns glittering in the sunlight.

The Rainbow Birds flew down to join their friends. As they landed in a flurry of welcoming squawks and whinnies, Ella landed the jeep on the grass nearby.

"This is incredible!" breathed Mia, gazing at the unusual birds and animals in awe. She loved all animals, but she'd never seen creatures like this before!

"Just wait until you meet the Tabbies," said Ella. She waved her wand, and a family

of giant cats came padding out from a nearby cluster of palm trees. They were as big as lions but their coats were fluffy and tabby-coloured. They walked towards them, their long tails swinging. "Why don't you give them a pat?" Ella suggested.

The Tabbies gave loud, rumbling purrs as Mia and Charlotte ran their hands through their coats.

"Oh! They're so soft!" said Charlotte.

"I love it here!" said Mia, looking like she was in heaven. One of the Tabbies purred loudly again as she rubbed behind its ears.

"Hey, Mia," Charlotte said. "What do you think a Tabby's favourite colour is?"

"What?" asked Mia.

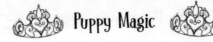

"Purrrr-ple, of course!" Charlotte said.

Mia giggled.

The unicorns came over to see the girls, too, staring at them with their beautiful, dark eyes.

"Would you like to give the unicorns a treat?" asked Ella. "They love apples." She waved her wand and suddenly the girls were holding apples in their hands.

Charlotte offered her apple to a unicorn, and giggled when its lips nuzzled her palm.

SQUAWK! A green parrot swooped down from the sky. It had a curved beak and black beady eyes.

"What type of bird is that?" Mia asked curiously, looking at the parrot.

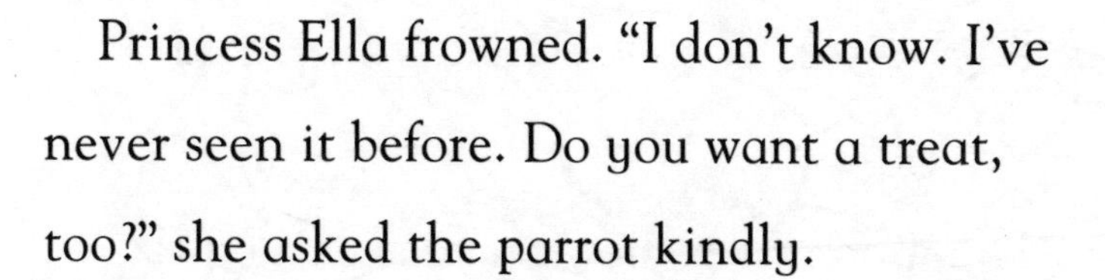

Princess Ella frowned. "I don't know. I've never seen it before. Do you want a treat, too?" she asked the parrot kindly.

She held her wand up, about to make a wish, but the parrot grabbed it in its sharp beak! Ella tried to pull it back, but the parrot wouldn't let go. "My wand!' Princess Ella cried as the parrot flew up into the sky again. "It's stolen my wand!"

The parrot perched in one of the palm trees. It moved the wand from its beak into one of its claws and squawked triumphantly. The green bird bobbed its head up and down and cackled. "Secret Princesses are frilly! Secret Princesses are silly!"

"What a horrible bird," said Charlotte.

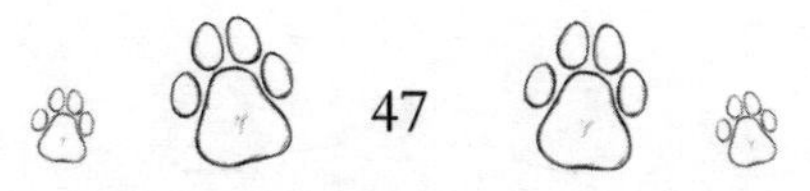

"I have to get my wand back," said Ella anxiously. The Secret Princesses' wands were their most magical possessions.

"I'll get it back for you," said Charlotte, running over to the tree.

The parrot gave her a mocking look. "Princess Poison wears green!"

It screeched nastily and flapped up to a higher branch. "She loves being mean!"

Princess Poison! Charlotte stopped, feeling as if she'd just had a bucket of icy water thrown over her. "The parrot knows Princess Poison!" she called to Ella and Mia.

The parrot cocked its head on one side and cawed:

"I have got a message to sing,
This wand will now unhappiness bring.
Princess Poison will use it to break
Any animal wishes people make.
And the animals here will feel
unhappy and sad
Because Princess Poison just
loves being bad!"

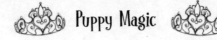

With a cackle, the parrot rose into the air and flew away – with Princess Ella's wand clutched tightly in its claws!

CHAPTER FOUR

A Magic Message

"It's taking my wand to Princess Poison!" gasped Ella as the parrot flapped away. "She's going to use it to ruin people's wishes!" Her brown eyes filled with tears. "This is awful!"

"Come back, you thief!" Charlotte yelled. But the parrot was already flying far away, out of sight.

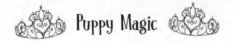

"Don't be upset, we'll help you get your wand back," said Mia, putting her arm round Princess Ella's shoulders.

Princess Ella dabbed her eyes. "You don't understand! If Princess Poison uses my wand to spoil someone's wish, I'll be banished from Wishing Star Palace, just like her."

Charlotte and Mia exchanged worried looks. They couldn't let that happen to Princess Ella.

Charlotte looked around the pool in dismay. The feathers on the flamingoes had dulled to a mustard yellow, the Rainbow Birds had shut their tails, silver tears rolled from the unicorns' dark eyes and the Tabbies had flopped listlessly to the ground.

"It's just like that horrible parrot said," said Mia in alarm. "All the animals here at Wishing Star Palace are unhappy and sad."

"We have to get the wand back!" said Charlotte. She thought fast. "I know. As soon as the Magic Mirror shows us someone with an animal wish, one that Ella would normally grant, Mia and I can go and help. Princess Poison is sure to come along and try to spoil it. She always does. When we see her, we'll find a way to get your wand back."

"That's very brave of you," said Princess Ella, looking worried. "But you'll have to be very careful. You know how nasty Princess Poison can be. She's not going to give up my wand without a fight."

"We don't care!" said Charlotte bravely. "We've beaten her before and we'll beat her again!"

"We will," Mia declared, grabbing her hand. "After all, we are training to be Friendship Princesses."

Friendship Princesses were rare and powerful Secret Princesses whose special talent was friendship. They always worked in pairs. Mia and Charlotte were the first trainee Friendship Princesses in over a hundred years.

"Mia's right. If we work together we can do anything," said Charlotte. "We'll grant any wishes that need granting and we'll get your wand back!"

Ella smiled at them. "Thank you. That's so kind of you. We'd better go back to the palace and tell everyone what's going on."

"Will the jeep be able to fly without your wand?" Mia asked. It would be a long walk back to the palace.

"Don't worry," said Ella. "I can't make the jeep fly but I can use my princess slippers to transport us." She pointed to her sparkling ruby shoes. "Take us to Wishing Star Palace!" she cried, taking the girls' hands and clicking her heels together.

All of a sudden, glittery blue magic lifted them all up and spun them away. Round and round they twirled as the grounds whizzed past beneath them. *This is so cool!* Charlotte thought with a rush of excitement. She couldn't wait to have magic slippers of her very own – but first they needed to grant four more wishes!

Ella's magical slippers set them all gently down inside the grand entrance hall.

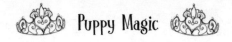

When the other princesses saw Mia and Charlotte, they hurried over to greet them.

Princess Ella quickly explained to everyone what had happened. All the other princesses gasped when they heard about her wand. "But Mia and Charlotte will try to stop Princess Poison," Ella said.

"We'll try to get the wand back when we next granting someone's animal wish," Mia explained.

Princess Sophie squeezed Mia's hand. "That's really brave of you, but are you sure? You know how horrible Princess Poison is."

"We don't care. We want to go," said Charlotte, looking at Mia who nodded firmly in agreement.

"After all, we have to start earning our rubies so we can get our own slippers," Mia said. Suddenly, her eyes widened. "Look!" she cried, pointing.

All of the princesses' wands were starting to light up. First one, then another, until they were all glowing.

"There must be a message in the Magic Mirror!" said Princess Ella. "Quick! Let's go and see what it says!"

Mia and Charlotte followed her swiftly up the curving stairs. The Magic Mirror was kept in a circular room at the top of one of the turrets. It was a large oval mirror on a tarnished gold stand.

The girls and Ella ran into the room.

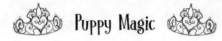

There was a message swirling across the mirror's glass. Charlotte read it out:

"The next stage of your training is about to begin
Four sparkling rubies you now must win.
Grant four wishes, however you choose,
Work together and earn your princess shoes."

She touched the mirror and the writing immediately faded, being replaced by the image of a slim girl with fair, curly hair. She was hugging a golden puppy and looking very worried. As they watched, she buried her head in the dog's soft fur and he licked her nose.

"Oh!" exclaimed Princess Ella. "That girl must have an animal wish."

"Don't worry," said Mia. "We'll help her."

Charlotte's heart pitter-pattered against her ribs.

Suddenly more swirly writing appeared.

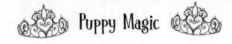

Charlotte read it out:

"A wish needs granting, adventures await,
Call Tessa's name, don't hesitate."

Mia looked at Charlotte. They both knew what they had to do.

"Tessa!" they cried in unison. Light swirled round in the mirror, going faster and faster until it formed a glowing tunnel. Gasping in excitement, Mia and Charlotte whooped as they felt themselves being pulled into the tunnel and whisked away. They couldn't wait to do more magic!

CHAPTER FIVE

The Naughty Puppy

Charlotte and Mia slid down the tunnel of light and whizzed out at the other end, landing on soft grass. Laughter and happy shouts filled Charlotte's ears. Feeling the warm sunshine on her bare legs, she realised that her princess dress had magically transformed into dress and a stripy top. Opening her eyes, she saw that they had

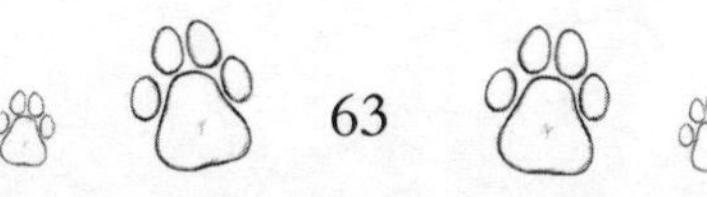

arrived in a park. There were children playing football and riding their bikes, toddlers feeding the ducks at the pond and parents pushing buggies and chatting. But thanks to the Secret Princess magic, no one at the park had noticed their sudden arrival.

Mia glanced round. "I wonder where Tessa is and why she's unhappy. Whoa!" She gasped as a young Labrador dog barrelled into her legs, almost knocking her over. He was still a puppy, with yellow fur, long gangly legs, floppy ears and eyes the colour of milk chocolate.

"It's the dog from the mirror!" Mia whispered to Charlotte. She stroked the dog and he licked her hands and wagged his tail.

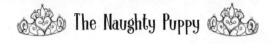

"You're lovely!" Mia said, crouching down and getting a lick on the nose that made her giggle. "What's your name?"

"And where's your owner?" Charlotte said, patting his back but keeping her face well away. She liked dogs, but not quite as much as Mia did – she didn't want her nose covered with wet doggy kisses!

"Baxter! Come back!" The girl from the mirror came hurrying across the grass, her long curls bouncing on her shoulders. Her tanned cheeks flushed as she reached Mia and Charlotte. "Sorry! I hope he's not bothering you. He's just a puppy and he's not very well-behaved yet."

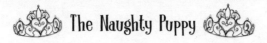

The puppy gambolled away from her and then jumped up at Mia.

"Baxter!" the girl said in dismay as he left paw prints on Mia's leggings.

"Don't worry, I love dogs," Mia said, taking hold of his collar. Baxter rolled on his back, asking for his tummy to be tickled.

"I help walk my auntie's dogs," Mia added. "I wish I could have a dog of my own but I don't think Flossie, my cat, would like that very much."

"Cats are lovely, but I think dogs are even better," said the girl. "Even when they don't do what they're told." She smiled at them. "I'm Tessa, by the way."

"I'm Charlotte and this is Mia," said Charlotte. She watched Tessa carefully. She had looked very upset when they had seen her in the mirror. What could be the problem?

"Are you here at the park with friends?" Charlotte asked, trying to find out more. They had to find out what Tessa's wish was!

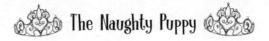

"No, just with my mum and dad and little brother," said Tess. She sighed and clipped Baxter's lead on. "Oh, Baxter," she said, dropping to her knees and hugging him. "You really have to try and be good. You have to pass your obedience test today."

"Even if he doesn't pass today, he'll probably pass it when he gets a bit older," said Mia encouragingly. "Sometimes it takes a while for puppies to settle down."

Tessa sighed. "The thing is I really need him to be good *now*. We're going on holiday next week, and Mum and Dad have said Baxter can only come if he proves that he can be good. Otherwise, he has to stay in a boarding kennel while we go away."

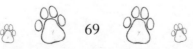

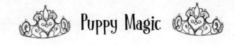

She bent over and kissed the naughty puppy on the top of his head. "I know he'll be sad at kennels without us and I won't be able to enjoy the holiday without him. Oh, I just wish he could behave well enough to pass his puppy training test so he can come on holiday with us!"

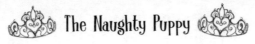

Charlotte and Mia looked at each other over the top of Tessa's head. So that was her wish!

"Maybe we can help," said Mia.

"Yes, we could help you and Baxter practise," said Charlotte.

Tessa's eyes lit up. "That would be great. The test is here in the park later this afternoon."

"We'd better get practising straight away then!" said Mia. Baxter spotted a squirrel scampering across the grass. With a delighted *woof* he pulled his lead out of Tessa's hand and bounded after it.

"Baxter! Come back!" called Tessa, but the puppy ignored her. She ran after him.

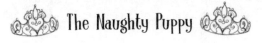

"It looks like we've got some work to do!" Charlotte whispered to Mia. They hurried after Tessa. She caught up with Baxter by the tree the squirrel had run up. The puppy was barking loudly in excitement. A few nearby people tutted and Tessa's cheeks flamed red with embarrassment.

She picked up Baxter and walked away.

"Why don't we find somewhere quiet to practise?" said Mia. She saw a good spot in the shade of some trees. "How about there?"

"OK, I'll just tell Mum and Dad where I'm going," said Tessa.

Charlotte and Mia waited while she ran over to where a man and woman were taking it in turns to push a toddler on a swing.

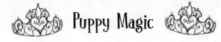

She spoke to them quickly and ran back. "They said it's fine," she said. "The test starts in an hour."

One hour! Charlotte took a deep breath as she looked at the naughty puppy. Oh dear. That wasn't much time at all!

CHAPTER SIX

Tennis Trouble

Baxter dragged Tessa over to the trees.

"Do you think we should use some wish magic?" Charlotte whispered to Mia. "If we just wished that Baxter was obedient, that would solve the problem."

Mia rubbed her nose. "But we can't grant a big wish like that."

Charlotte knew Mia was right. Their

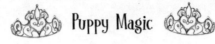

magic wasn't powerful enough to grant one big wish – instead they could use three smaller wishes to help people.

"Besides, I think we might be able to help Tessa without magic," Mia went on. "I went to dog training classes with my auntie and I can remember lots of things that we were taught to do." She raised her voice. "Why don't you show us what Baxter's been learning in his lessons," she called to Tessa.

"OK, well, we've been teaching the dogs to sit and lie down," said Tessa. She stood up straight. "Sit, Baxter!"

Baxter just wagged his tail and looked at them, his tongue hanging out as he gave a big doggy grin.

"Sit!" she insisted. Tessa tried to push his bottom down, but he thought she wanted to play and he frolicked around.

"Oh, this is no good!" Tessa said in dismay. "If I can't even get him to sit, he's got no chance of passing."

Charlotte looked hopefully at Mia.

"Have you got any dog treats with you?" Mia asked Tessa.

Tessa nodded and took out a plastic bag with some bits of sausage in. "Helen, our instructor, says it's easier to train puppies if you use food. Baxter loves hot dogs!"

"WOOF!" said Baxter, licking his lips when he saw the treats.

"You can only have a treat if you're good," Mia told him. She took a piece of hot dog, then holding the treat above his nose she moved it slowly back over his head. Baxter's eyes followed it. "Sit!" said Mia, giving him the sausage as his bottom hit the ground. She repeated the command a few times, then got Tessa to try.

Baxter quickly got the idea that if he sat he would get a treat and soon he was sitting when he heard the command.

Next, Mia used the treats to teach him to lie down, bringing the treat down to the ground between his paws and saying 'down'.

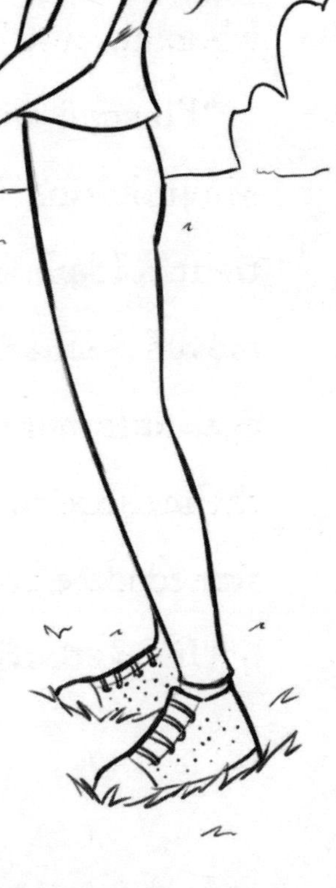

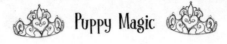

"You're brilliant at dog training!" said Tessa, as Baxter quickly started to lie down.

"I just love being with animals," said Mia. "When I'm older I want to be a vet, or maybe someone who trains animals for films."

"Can you help me to get him to walk to heel?" Tessa said. "He always pulls on his lead."

"I'll try," said Mia. She thought about the problem. "Why don't you use some more treats? Try holding one close to your leg."

"OK," said Tessa eagerly. "I'll try it." She got some more treats out. "Heel, Baxter!"

Smelling the treat in her hand, Baxter stayed close to her leg.

"It's working!" said Charlotte.

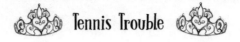

"I've got an idea!" said Mia. "Make it a game. If you pretend you're trying to run away from him, I bet he'll be even more keen to stay with you."

Tessa ran around, twisting and turning as if she was trying to get away. Baxter bounced along beside her, his tail wagging happily. He didn't try to pull away once. Tessa stopped, her eyes shining, and fed him a sausage. "Oh, this is going so well. Thank you for helping me!"

"Oi! You girls!" They turned round and saw a small, tubby man approaching them, bouncing a ball on a tennis racket. He was wearing white shorts and his white shirt was stretched tight over his round tummy.

He had a baseball cap pulled down over his face. "Do you girls know where the tennis courts are?"

Charlotte frowned. The man's voice sounded very familiar.

"The courts are just over that way," said Tessa, pointing. She held on to Baxter tightly. He was watching the ball eagerly.

"Oh, good. I have a feeling I'm going to have a real ball today playing tennis!" The little man chuckled. "Starting right now!" He hit the ball hard towards the nearby flowerbed with his tennis racket.

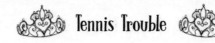

"WOOF!" Baxter pulled free from Tessa and raced after the ball. He leapt over the railings and landed in the neat flowerbed.

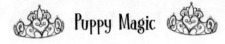

He started digging around, trying to find the ball, sending flowers and dirt flying.

"Baxter, come here!" cried Tessa.

"Dearie me, your dog is very badly behaved, isn't he?" said the man. "The park warden isn't going to be happy when he sees him in the flowerbed. He'll make you and your dog leave the park." He gave a mean snigger. "Won't that be a shame?"

Tessa turned to Mia and Charlotte. "I have to get Baxter out of there! If we're kicked out of the park he won't be able to do his puppy test."

"Quick!" said Mia, running towards the flowerbed with Tessa.

"Now where's the warden?" said the man.

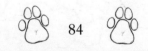

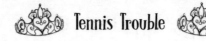

As he spoke again, Charlotte suddenly realised who it was.

"Hex!" she cried. Hex was Princess Poison's mean servant. "You hit that ball into the flowers on purpose!" she said angrily.

"Of course I did!" Hex said gleefully. "My mistress is going to ruin that girl's wish.

Her dog won't be able to go on holiday with her and she'll be all sad. *Boo hoo! Boo hoo!*" He pretended to cry but his little eyes gleamed brightly. "And best of all, you two won't become Secret Princesses!"

"Oh, yes we will!" said Charlotte angrily. "You and Princess Poison won't stop us from granting Tessa's wish!" She made a grab for him but he jumped out of the way.

"Can't stop me!" he cried, running towards the park warden, waving his arms. "Warden! Warden, over here! There's a dog ruining your flowerbeds."

Charlotte watched in dismay as she saw the park warden look over in their direction. They had to do something – and quickly!

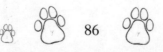

She raced to the flowerbed. Tessa and Mia were trying to haul Baxter out, but he was still scrabbling at the flowers. Clods of soil and loose petals now covered the grass outside the railings. "Baxter! Get out of there right now!" Tessa panted.

"The warden's coming!" Charlotte gasped.

Mia glanced over her shoulder and saw Hex and the park warden heading their way.

"That man in the tennis kit is Hex," Charlotte hissed. "He's trying to get Baxter banned from the park."

"What are we going to do?" said Mia as Tessa finally dragged Baxter out. His paws and tongue were muddy, so it was clear that the naughty puppy was the one who had caused all the mess.

Charlotte lifted her chin and held her pendant. It was glowing like a beam of sunshine. "Now it's time for some Wish Magic!" she said.

CHAPTER SEVEN

Flowery Magic!

Mia pulled out her own half-heart pendant. The girls pressed their pendants together so that they made a perfect heart shape. Light sparkled over their fingers making their skin tingle. "I wish that the flowerbed would look lovely!" whispered Charlotte.

There was a flash of bright light and the flowerbed was filled with beautiful flowers!

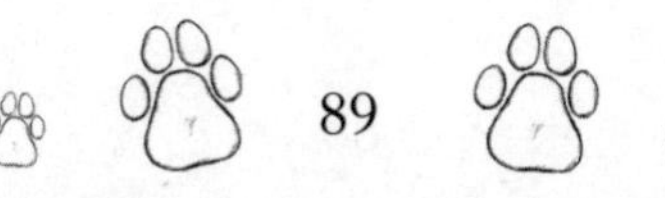

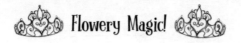

Instead of just having neat rows of pink and red begonias, it was filled with flowers of all different sizes, shapes and colours. There were huge white daisies, tall spikes of blue, bell-shaped blooms, clouds of pink roses and in the centre there was a green bush trimmed in the shape of a Rainbow Bird, with a beautiful leafy tail.

Baxter woofed in surprise and Tessa's mouth fell open. "What just happened?" She looked at the girls with startled eyes. "What's going on?"

"We'll tell you in a minute," said Charlotte, hearing voices behind them. She swung round. Hex was pulling the park warden towards the flowerbed.

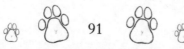

"Yes, over this way, warden! Come and see what that pesky dog has done. It should be banned from the park! Look!" he said triumphantly, pointing at the flowerbed.

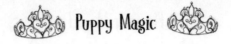

The warden peered around him and paused. "Um ... I'm sorry, sir, but the flowerbed looks in perfect order," he said.

"What?" Hex stared at the beautiful flowerbed. "No!" he exclaimed. "That dog was digging the flowers up. I saw it!"

The warden looked at Buster, who was sitting obediently beside Tessa. "You must be mistaken. This dog looks very well behaved."

"Gah!" exclaimed Hex angrily. Charlotte and Mia couldn't help giggling at his cross face.

"Come along, sir," said the warden. "Let's leave these girls in peace."

As the warden led him away, Hex shook his fist. "I'll get you back for this!" he hissed.

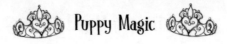

"You think you've ruined my mistress's plan, don't you? Well, she's only just got started. She'll stop you yet!"

Charlotte and Mia exchanged looks.

"OK," said Tessa, looking at the girls in confusion. "What's going on?"

Charlotte took a breath. This was always a tricky part of their adventures. "Tessa," she said slowly. "Mia and I have to tell you something. We're trainee Secret Princesses."

"Princesses?" Tessa stared at them as if they were crazy.

"Our job is to try and make people happy," Mia explained quickly.

"By using magic and granting special wishes," added Charlotte.

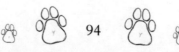

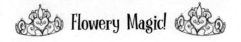

Tessa's mouth opened and shut as if she didn't know what to say. She stared at the girls in amazement.

"I know it's hard to believe," said Mia gently, "but it's true. We came here to help you. Our necklaces let us grant three wishes – we just used the first one to fix the flowerbed."

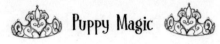

"But why didn't the warden notice it was so different?" asked Tessa.

"That's all part of the magic," said Charlotte. "You'll notice, but no one else will. It has to be kept a secret."

"So, you're here to help Baxter pass his puppy test so he can come on holiday with me?" Tessa asked.

Mia and Charlotte nodded. "We'll do whatever we can," said Charlotte. "But there's something else you need to know. There's a mean person called Princess Poison who is trying to stop us. That man was her servant, Hex. They always try to stop any wishes from coming true because it makes them more powerful."

"But we won't let them stop us," said Mia.

"OK," said Tessa slowly.

"We'll watch out for them trying any more nasty tricks," said Charlotte. "But for now, let's get on with training Baxter."

Tessa patted the puppy. "He was being good, wasn't he?"

"Really good," said Mia. "Now you need to practise calling him back. I bet they'll make you do that in the puppy test."

Tessa nodded. "It's the thing he's worst at. Have you got any ideas of what I can do?"

"Why don't you use the hot dogs again?" said Charlotte. "If you show him that you've got them, he's bound to want to come and get a treat."

"And maybe if you make your voice sound really exciting it will help," said Mia. "Make him think it's a game again."

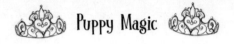

They set to work. Tessa did exactly what Mia and Charlotte had suggested. When she called Baxter, she held out a piece of sausage.

Baxter raced over to her every time and then she gave him lots of cuddles and praise.

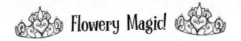

"I think he's starting to get the idea!" said Charlotte, as Tessa managed to get further and further away and still call Baxter back. "You're doing a great job!"

SQUAWK! A green bird swooped down from the sky and landed on Tessa's head. She squealed in shock.

"It's Princess Poison's parrot!" gasped Charlotte, recognising the bird who had stolen Ella's wand. Baxter started to bark angrily at the parrot.

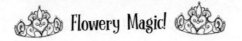

"Secret Princesses won't win! Secret Princesses won't win!" the parrot squawked.

Tessa dropped the lead and tried to push the bird off her head.

The parrot screeched in delight and let go of her hair. It swooped down in front of Baxter's nose and then flew away, off across the park.

"WOOF!" Baxter barked and gave chase.

"Baxter, stop!" cried Tessa.

"Baxter, come here!" Mia called desperately, but Baxter ignored her too. Following the parrot, he dashed around a group of mums and toddlers playing on the grass, and right through the bandstand where some musicians were busy setting up.

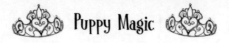

He jumped over a set of drums and raced across the path, almost knocking a teenager off his bike as he chased the parrot.

"Oh no!" cried Charlotte in alarm. "Quick! We've got to stop him. Run!"

CHAPTER EIGHT

Panic in the Park

The parrot flew towards the tennis court and landed on one of the nets.

"Woof!" Baxter bounded on to the court, knocking into a tennis player. He leapt at the bird but it soared up into the air and flew around and around the court. Baxter chased after it, barking happily. He thought it was all a game!

"Sorry!" gasped Tessa to the tennis players as she ran after him. "I'm really sorry! Oh, please, Baxter, come here!"

"That dog should be on a lead!" shouted one man, crossly.

Charlotte dodged past them. Baxter had stopped and was now watching the parrot as it perched on a nearby tree.

Charlotte dived forward and tried to grab him, but the naughty little puppy bounded out of reach and raced away.

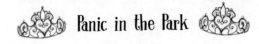

"Charlotte! He's heading for the swimming pool!" cried Mia.

There were lots of children in the pool, splashing in their bright swimming costumes.

Eyes fixed on the parrot, Baxter leapt into the pool. Water flew into the air. The kids pointed at Baxter and laughed as he wagged his tail and sprayed water everywhere. One little boy fell over and started to cry. The lifeguard blew his whistle.

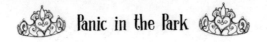

Charlotte, Mia and Tessa watched Baxter splash through the water. The parrot had reached the sandpit and landed on a bench beside it. It squawked tauntingly.

Baxter jumped out of the pool, shook, then leapt into the sand and grabbed a plastic spade. He ran round with it in his mouth as parents shouted and children shrieked.

"He's off again!" gasped Tessa as Baxter dropped the spade and charged after the smirking green parrot as it flapped past the café, heading towards the entrance to the park.

"Oh, no! If Baxter goes through the gate he'll get on to the road!" cried Mia in alarm. "We have to stop him!"

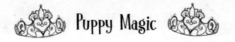

Charlotte sprinted after him. Her heart pounded as she ran. What were they going to do? Baxter was almost at the entrance.

In a few seconds he would be out on the road. She grabbed her pendant desperately. But Mia was now too far away for them to put their half-hearts together and make magic.

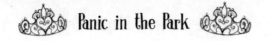

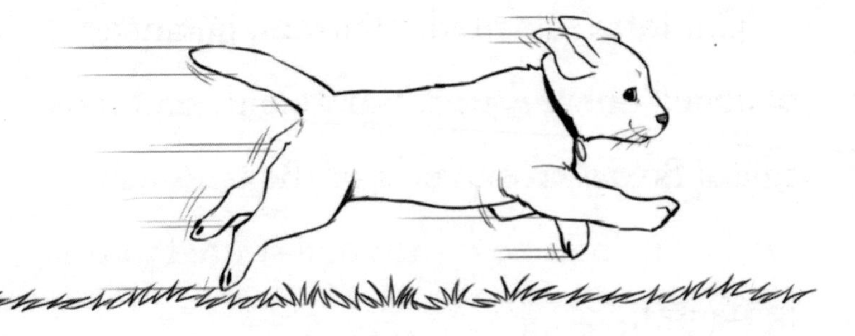

From behind her, Charlotte heard Mia shout, "No, Baxter!" Her voice rang with authority. "Baxter! Come!" The puppy slowed and looked at back at her. "Come here!" Mia said. She began to pretend she had something exciting in her hand. "What's this? Come and see what I've got!" she said in a high-pitched voice.

Charlotte joined in. "Yummy, yummy, yummy!" she tempted him. "Come and get this delicious treat, Baxter!" Baxter's ears pricked up and he turned and started to trot in their direction.

"He's coming!" said Charlotte in delight.

"Phew!" sighed Tessa in relief as Baxter ran towards them, away from the road.

But just as Charlotte reached out for his collar, the puppy caught sight of the nearby café. He looked at the people sitting at tables eating ice creams and his tail wagged.

"Uh oh," said Mia.

"WOOF!" Baxter barked greedily, bounding towards the café. Reaching the nearest table, he put his paws on it and

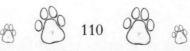

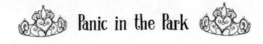

licked an ice cream that a lady was holding!

"Hey!" the lady cried. Looking very pleased with himself, Baxter gobbled it up in one mouthful and then bounded towards the next table and jumped up. People shouted at him and tried to push him away, but he

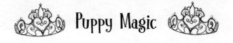

knocked the table over and licked up their ice creams from the floor. Charlotte ran over and grabbed his collar.

"Got you!" she cried in relief. But then she looked around at all the cross faces and her heart sank.

"I'm going to get the warden!" shouted one of the mums.

"That dog is a menace!" shouted one of the dads.

Charlotte looked around at the chaos of cross parents, overturned tables, spilled ice creams and crying children, and held Baxter while Tessa clipped his lead back on. Then she went over to her best friend. "We've got to do something, Mia."

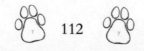

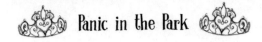

"There's only one way to sort this out," Mia said.

Charlotte nodded. If there was ever a time for some wish magic it was now!

She and Mia fitted their pendants together.

"I wish that everything was fixed – and everyone was eating their favourite ice creams!" whispered Mia.

There was a flash of light. In the blink of an eye, everything was neat again and everyone was sitting down, smiling, and tucking into knickerbocker glories, banana splits, ice cream sundaes and enormous cones. Mia, Charlotte and Tessa found huge ice creams before them, topped with delicious sprinkles.

"It worked!' said Mia, looking around.

"And we got ice cream too!" said Charlotte. "Yum, honeycomb and strawberry, my two favourite flavours!"

"And I've got chocolate and cherry!" said Mia, licking her lips.

Tessa stared round. "Nobody's acting like anything strange has happened at all."

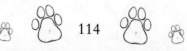

"We told you," Mia said, taking a big bite of her ice cream. "The magic stops people noticing when wishes happen."

Tessa breathed a sigh of relief and licked her caramel swirl ice cream. "They've forgotten about Baxter being naughty, too."

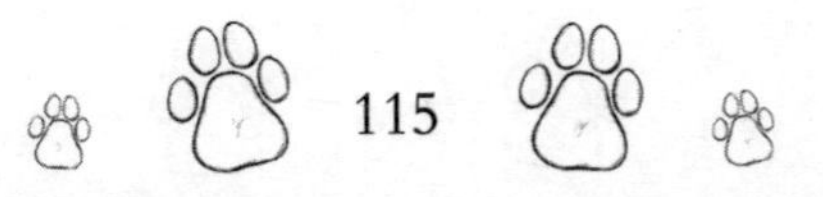

The girls ate up their delicious ice creams and then Tessa checked the time. "I'd better get a move on. It's almost time for puppy class to start," she said. "He'll probably fail his test, though."

"Don't say that," said Mia. "He was really good when we were practising earlier."

"Princess Poison's parrot distracted him," said Charlotte. "Well, that and the sight of ice cream! But if we see that parrot again we'll chase it far away."

Mia squeezed Tessa's hand comfortingly.

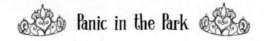

"You can do it. Just use your treats and make a big fuss of him when he does something right," she said.

Tessa took a deep breath. "OK. I'll try."

They finished their ice creams and then they headed over to where a group of puppies were gathering on a large roped-off section of grass with their owners. There was a sign saying 'Preston Park Puppy Class'." The lady in charge was wearing a navy tracksuit and carrying a clipboard.

"That's Helen, she runs the class," Tessa told Mia and Charlotte.

Helen spotted her. "Ah, there's Baxter! Come along and join the others."

"Good luck!" Mia said.

"We'll be cheering you on from here," Charlotte said, as she and Mia joined Tessa's parents and little brother, who were standing at the edge of the roped-off area.

Tessa shot them a grateful look and led Baxter into the ring to join the other puppies. They were all really cute – there was a French bulldog, a little Jack Russell

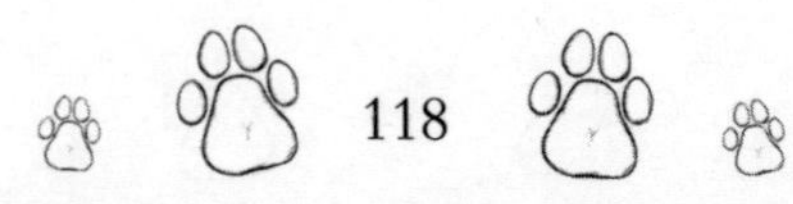

terrier and a sausage dog. Charlotte grinned at Mia, who looked like she wished she could go and cuddle them all! The sausage dog wagged its tail happily and rushed over to play with Baxter.

Charlotte nudged Mia. "Why are Dalmatians no good at hide and seek?" she asked her friend.

"Why?" said Mia.

"Because they're always spotted!" Charlotte giggled.

Mia shook her head and groaned.

"I think it's time for us to get started," Helen said.

"This is it," Mia whispered. "It's Baxter's big moment."

They watched anxiously. Was he going to pass the test and make Tessa's wish come true? Or was Tessa going to have to go on holiday without him?

"Find a space, everyone!" called Helen. "And let's begin!"

"Make way! Make way!" called a harsh, bossy voice. "We're coming through. We want to take the test!"

The girls looked round as two figures pushed their way into the class. One of them was a tall, thin woman with an ice-blonde streak in her jet-black hair. She was dressed in a bright green tracksuit and high heels.

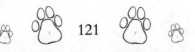

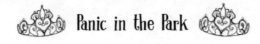

A big, muscular dog walked beside her on a lead. He had a squashed-up face and was wearing a green collar with a skull and crossbones on it. As he looked at the other puppies, his lip curled up and he snarled. A short fat man in tennis clothes was scurrying along behind them, carrying a pink, grumpy-looking poodle.

Charlotte squeaked in alarm. “It’s Princess Poison and Hex! And that’s Miss Fluffy.” She recognised the poodle from their last adventure, when Princess Poison and Hex had tried to stop a girl named Sam from winning a TV talent show.

“What are they doing here?” said Mia, giving a groan.

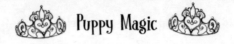

"They're going to try to ruin things as usual, I bet," said Charlotte grimly. "But we're not going to let them!"

CHAPTER NINE

The Puppy Test

"Are you in charge?" Princess Poison said, peering down her nose at Helen. "We're here for the test."

"But you haven't come to any of the puppy training classes," Helen protested. "In fact, your pets aren't even puppies any more, they're much too old. I'm afraid you're going to have to come to a different class."

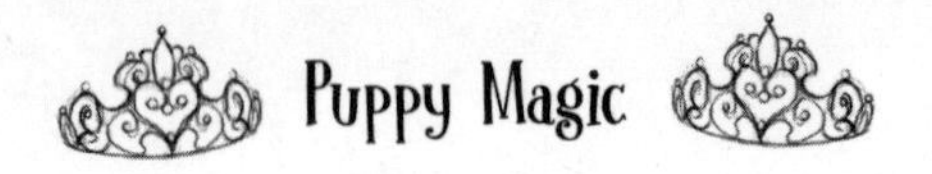

Charlotte saw Princess Poison pull out Ella's wand and flick it behind her back. The two dogs were instantly transformed into puppies! Miss Fluffy was tiny and even fluffier, and the bulldog was sweet, even though it still had a cross look on its wrinkly face.

A confused look came over Helen's face. She looked around and blinked several times. "So, you say you're here to take the puppy test?" she said. "Of course. Silly me. I must have forgotten."

"Yes, that's right," said Princess Poison, silkily. "You forgot all about us, but now we're here and you're going to let us join in."

"Princess Poison's put a spell on Helen!" Mia whispered to Charlotte.

"And she used Ella's wand," Charlotte whispered back. "I recognise the paw print on the end of it."

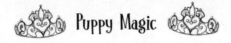

"What are your dogs called?" Helen asked.

Princess Poison pulled her bulldog puppy forward. "This is Crusher." He snarled at Helen and she took a hasty step backwards.

Hex waved Miss Fluffy's paw. "And this is ickle wittle Miss Fluffy!" he said in a silly, whiny voice.

"Miss Fluffy and er … Crusher," said Helen faintly. She wrote their names down on her clipboard. "OK, well why don't you join the others? We're going to start by asking the puppies to sit and lie down."

"This is awful," whispered Mia to Charlotte as Princess Poison headed towards Tessa. "We can't let Princess Poison join in with the class."

"I don't see how we can stop her," said Charlotte. They could hardly march over and demand that Princess Poison left. "But at least now we'll have a chance to get Ella's wand back."

Mia nodded. "We just have to make sure she doesn't stop Baxter passing his test."

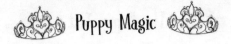

Princess Poison saw the girls watching her and wiggled her fingers at them, smiling smugly. Charlotte glared back at her.

Baxter went to say hello to Crusher, Princess Poison's dog.

"GRRRR!" Crusher snarled.

Baxter backed off so hastily that he bumped right into Miss Fluffy. She yapped furiously and snapped at his tail. He spun round in alarm and hid behind Tessa's legs, whining softly.

"It looks like someone needs to learn how to keep their dog under control," snapped Princess Poison. She pointed to Baxter and called to Helen. "I think this dog should be expelled from the class."

To Charlotte's relief, Helen looked shocked. "No one's going to be expelled," she said. "Why don't we get started? Can you all get your dogs to sit next to you, please?"

Baxter glanced anxiously at the two mean dogs on either side of him. Tessa gave him a reassuring pat, but his tail had stopped wagging. It hung low between his legs and his ears were flattened nervously against his head.

"Oh, poor Baxter," said Mia. "Do you see his tail? It means he's frightened."

"Ready, everyone!" called Helen. "You have ten seconds to get your dog to sit!"

"Baxter, sit!" said Tessa. Baxter started to sit down but, as he did so, Miss Fluffy darted

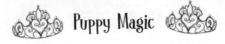

forward and nipped his tail. Baxter yelped loudly and jumped up.

Hex giggled in delight.

“Did you see that?’ said Charlotte, clutching Mia’s arm.

“It was SO mean!” Mia said angrily.

“Sit!” Tessa cried hastily. Luckily Baxter quickly plonked his bottom on the ground just as Helen looked up from her stopwatch. She made a tick on her clipboard.

Tessa gave a sigh of relief as Baxter sat at her feet obediently. Despite Princess Poison, Hex and their mean pets, Baxter was being really good.

"Yay!" cried Mia and Charlotte. Tessa's parents cheered, too.

Tessa exchanged relieved looks with the girls and crouched down to cuddle Baxter. He licked her face in delight.

On one side of them, Miss Fluffy was standing with her nose in the air. On the other side, Crusher was chasing his tail.

Next, Helen told everyone to make their dogs lie down.

"Come on, you can do it, Baxter!" Charlotte cried out.

Tessa stood between Baxter and the poodle, and Baxter lay down as soon as she gave him the command.

"Well done, everyone," said Helen when the exercise was finished. "Now for the next stage of the test. Give your dogs a walk round and then we'll test how good they are at staying and coming when called."

Charlotte gave Tessa a thumbs up as she and Baxter started walking around the ring.

"You're doing really well!" Mia called out as Tessa walked past.

"You again!" Princess Poison hissed, leading Crusher towards Mia and Charlotte. "Do you know why my dog is called Crusher?" She didn't wait for them to reply,

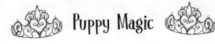

just pointed at Tessa. "Because he's going to crush that girl's dreams – and your chances of becoming Secret Princesses too!" She cackled. "That mutt of hers won't pass its silly test and then she won't be able to take him on holiday!"

Just then there was a squawk and the green parrot landed on her shoulder.

"Silly princesses!" it squawked. "Spoil wishes!"

"Yes, Venom, my darling, that's quite right," cooed Princess Poison, stroking its emerald-coloured feathers. "You've met Venom already, I believe?" she said, looking sharply at the girls. "I decided that if the Secret Princesses had pets, then why

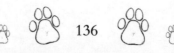

shouldn't I? And Venom has been very useful so far." She reached inside her tracksuit and pulled out Princess Ella's wand again. "All my pets obey when I tell them to 'Fetch!'" She sniggered. "Be sure to tell your princess friend that her wand is proving very useful.

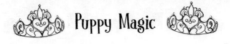

And, best of all, when I use it to spoil Tessa's wish, Ella will be banished from Wishing Star Palace for ever."

"We won't let you do that!" cried Mia.

Charlotte snatched at the wand. "Give that back!"

With a snarl, Crusher lunged at her.

"Watch out!" Mia pulled her back just as Crusher's puppy jaws snapped shut right where Charlotte's arm had been.

Mia turned furiously on Princess Poison. "You shouldn't be allowed to keep pets. You're cruel and you're training them to be horrible."

Princess Poison smirked. "You're right," she said gleefully. "I am! And if you two get

in my way, you'll see just how horrible they can be! Come, Crusher! Come, Venom!" Swinging round, she tottered away.

"OK, gather around, everyone!" Helen called. "Time to test how good your puppies are at staying."

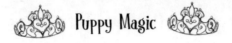

Charlotte turned shakily to Mia. "Thanks for saving me. Crusher almost bit me. It would have been much worse if he was his normal size."

"It was really brave of you to try and grab Ella's wand, but we can't get it like that," said Mia. "We'll have to try and get it another way."

They watched anxiously as Baxter lay down obediently. Tessa walked a few paces away, but as soon as Helen started the stopwatch, Venom swooped down in front of Baxter's nose.

Baxter's head jerked up and his ears pricked up.

"Stay!" Tessa cried. "Baxter, stay!"

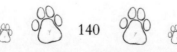

The puppy looked at her, hesitated, then put his nose on his paws and stayed still.

"Oh, good boy!" breathed Mia.

When Helen called that the time was up, Tessa ran back to Baxter and hugged him. "You were so good!" she praised him as he squirmed in delight and wagged his tail on the ground happily.

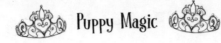

"Nearly done," called Helen. "We just need to test whether your puppies will come when they're called."

"Go on, Baxter!" called Charlotte.

"You know what to do!"

When it was Tessa's turn, she told Baxter to stay and went to the middle.

"Baxter! Baxter! Come!" called Tessa, getting a treat out. Baxter's ears pricked and he jumped up and raced over to her.

"Super!" Helen smiled as Tessa patted him.

"Baxter's doing really well. He just needs to show me he can walk round on a loose lead."

Tessa reached into her pocket for another treat. But Princess Poison pulled out Ella's wand again and pointed it towards Tessa's hand. Tessa gasped as the treat vanished into thin air. Charlotte and Mia saw her start to frantically check all her other pockets, but she clearly couldn't find anything in them.

"Princess Poison's made her treats vanish!" said Charlotte. "What's Tessa going to do?"

"It might be OK," said Mia. "Baxter's learnt so much already ..."

"Come on, Baxter," breathed Charlotte. "Be a good boy."

"OK, Tessa. Off you go," said Helen. "Just walk Baxter round the outside of the ring."

Tessa walked off, closing her fingers so Baxter couldn't see that she didn't have a treat. Baxter trotted at her side, nudging her closed fist hopefully with his nose.

"You can do it, Tessa!" Charlotte encouraged as Tessa walked past them again.

"Good dog, Baxter!" said Mia.

"Not for long!" a voice hissed from nearby. They looked round to see that Princess Poison had pulled out Ella's wand. "Baxter's been such a good dog he really does deserve a lovely treat," she said. "Hmm, now, what did you say he loves? Hot dogs, I think it was ..."

She flicked Ella's wand and a hot dog stand suddenly appeared just outside the ring. The delicious smell of freshly cooked hot dogs wafted towards them.

Baxter's eyes fixed on the hot dog stand and he stopped walking.

"Come on, Baxter!" said Tessa, giving a little tug on his lead. But he ignored her. Instead he licked his lips greedily and pulled on his lead, trying to get Tessa over to the stand. Princess Poison sniggered.

"No, Baxter! Heel!" Tessa said, her voice rising urgently.

Helen frowned and started making notes on her clipboard.

"We've got to do something!" Mia said.

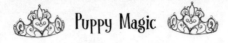

Baxter barked excitedly and pulled on his lead even more.

Charlotte pulled her pendant out. "We've got one wish left – let's use it!" she said.

CHAPTER TEN

Pass or Fail?

"I wish the hot dog stand would change into ... into a balloon stand!" whispered Mia as they touched their half-hearts together. There was a bright flash of light and then the pendants faded. The magic had all gone, but the wish had worked! The hot dog stand had changed into a stand with lots of helium balloons – including some shaped like dogs!

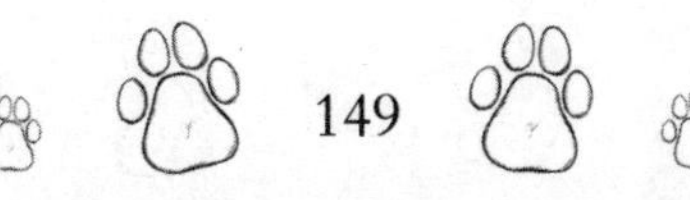

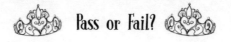

There was even a poodle like Miss Fluffy!

"A balloon stand?" Charlotte said in astonishment.

Mia shrugged and grinned sheepishly. "I couldn't think of anything else! At least it worked."

Baxter had lost interest in the stall now that it sold balloons and not yummy hot dogs. He started trotting along beside Tessa again. They completed a whole circle and then took their place back with the other puppies.

"It was an awesome idea!" said Charlotte, hugging Mia.

"Excellent work!" said Helen, marking a large tick on her clipboard. Tessa hugged

Baxter and grinned at the girls in relief.

"And now it's Miss Fluffy's turn," said Helen, consulting her list. But the pink poodle refused to move. No matter how hard Hex tugged the lead, she just stayed sitting. He reached for her collar and she growled at him.

"Oh dear," sighed Helen. "Let's try Crusher instead."

Princess Poison walked Crusher around the ring but halfway round, Crusher started barking ferociously at one of the other puppies. Princess Poison tugged and pulled at him but he just kept barking and growling. He only stopped when Venom landed on his back and pecked at his ears.

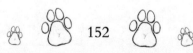

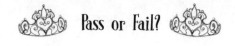

Helen marked a large cross on her sheet.

"That's it then. Now it's time for the results," she told the class. "I'm delighted to say that Candy, Daisy, Buster, Freddie, Simba and Baxter have all passed their tests. Well done to all of you! Please come and get your certificates."

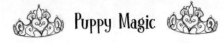

Mia and Charlotte whooped. Tessa looked delighted. “You did it, Baxter!” she cried. “Oh, you clever, clever dog!” He wagged his tail and licked her face.

“What about Miss Fluffy?” demanded Hex.

“Miss Fluffy and Crusher are two of the

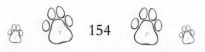

worst behaved dogs I have ever seen," said Helen. "They need to come to some more classes and learn to be better behaved."

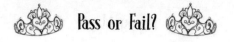

Crusher started to growl and Miss Fluffy yapped angrily.

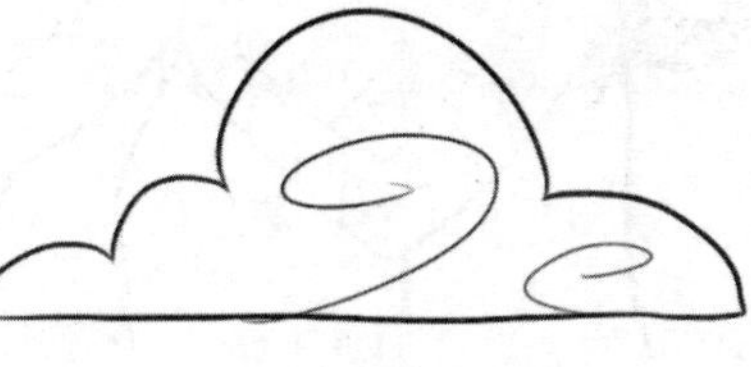

"That's not fair!" whined Hex.

"It doesn't matter. We didn't come here to get some silly certificate, you fool. We're leaving right this minute!" snapped Princess Poison, storming off.

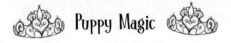

Hex followed, dragging Crusher and Miss Fluffy behind him.

Tessa's parents came hurrying over to congratulate Tessa as she collected her certificate from Helen.

"Baxter was *such* a good boy!" said Tessa's mum, grinning at Tessa.

"Good boy, Baxter! Good dog!" said Tessa's little brother, hugging him.

"So can he come on holiday with us?" Tessa asked hopefully.

Tessa's parents exchanged looks.

"Well, we did book a cottage that allows dogs ..." said Tessa's mum.

"And Baxter *would* love playing in the sea ..." said Tessa's dad.

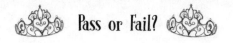

"He can come!" they said together, grinning.

"Really?" Tessa gasped in delight. "Oh, thank you! Did you hear that, Baxter? You're coming on holiday!" She glanced at Charlotte and Mia and beamed. "My wish has come true!"

Suddenly, there was a bright flash of light and all the helium balloons floated into the air. Dogs yapped excitedly and people pointed in delight as the brightly coloured

balloons floated up into the blue sky. The band at the bandstand burst into a lively song and a small plane flew by overhead with a banner saying "Congratulations!" trailing behind it.

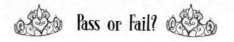

Charlotte squeezed Mia's hand excitedly. "We did it!" she said happily. "We granted Tessa's wish!"

"Thank you so much!" Tessa said, hugging Mia and Charlotte. "If it wasn't for you, Baxter would have failed. I'm so glad I met you."

"And we're glad we met you," said Mia. Baxter jumped up at her. "And you too, Baxter," she said, ruffling his ears.

"Have an amazing time on holiday," Charlotte told Tessa.

"Oh, I will!" she said joyfully.

Tessa's mum and dad called her. She said goodbye and ran to join her family with Baxter bounding beside her.

"This isn't over!" Holding Crusher's lead, Princess Poison stalked up to Charlotte and Mia, followed by Hex and Miss Fluffy.

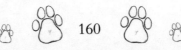

"You may have granted that silly wish … but I still have the wand!" Princess Poison snapped. "And you are never going to get it back."

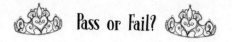

"Never!" echoed Hex triumphantly.

"You'll be sorry you ruined my plans today, very sorry indeed," said Princess Poison.

"I'm going to use Ella's wand to spoil wishes, and then there will be one less princess at Wishing Star Palace!" She reached inside her tracksuit for the wand.

Mia caught her breath, but Charlotte saw a stick on the ground and had a brilliant idea.

"Actually, I think you're the one who's going to be sorry!" she cried. Grabbing the stick, she ran towards the nearby pond and threw it as hard as she could. "Fetch!"

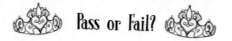

Crusher started to drag Princess Poison towards the water.

"Stop, you mutt! Stop!" Princess Poison screamed as he tugged her along.

But Crusher didn't listen. He was determined to fetch the stick that Charlotte had thrown. He leapt into the pond, pulling Princess Poison behind him! She disappeared under the water for a moment and then emerged, screeching in fury.

Water and pondweed dripped from her hair, and a frog sat on her head.

"Maybe you need a few more puppy training lessons?" Charlotte said with a laugh.

"And it looks like you've found another pet, Princess Poison," Mia said with a giggle, pointing at the frog.

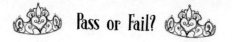

"Or you could wear him as a hat," said Charlotte. "He *toad*-ally suits you!"

"Gah!" Princess Poison shook her head and the frog plopped back into the water with a relieved croak.

"I'll get you for this!" Princess Poison hissed, pointing at the girls with a bony finger. She grabbed Crusher's lead and dragged him out of the pond. "Hex!" she shouted as she waded out of the water. "We're leaving!"

Hex scurried over with Miss Fluffy in his arms. "Of course, mistress!" he said anxiously.

Princess Poison fixed Charlotte and Mia with a furious look.

"Next time, you won't be so lucky. You mark my words! You'd better watch out for me and my pets!" She clapped her hands and then she, Hex and their horrible animals vanished in a puff of green smoke.

"We did it," Charlotte said, turning to Mia in delight. "We granted a wish and we stopped Princess Poison." She gave her friend a high five.

"Go, us!" Mia pointed at the pond.

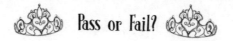

"Look! Something's happening!" A ripple of sparkles was shimmering on the water. The surface suddenly became as smooth as a mirror and an image appeared.

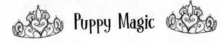

"Princess Ella!" said Charlotte.

Princess Ella waved at them. "I've been watching everything in the Magic Mirror. Well done! You've both been brilliant."

"We didn't get your wand back," said Mia sadly.

"But Princess Poison didn't spoil anyone's wish with it," said Princess Ella, with a smile.

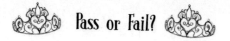

"And you made Tessa's wish come true, and that's the most important thing."

"We'll get it back next time," said Charlotte. "We won't let Princess Poison banish you."

"Thank you," Princess Ella said with a big smile. "Now, it's time for you to come back here. Just hold your necklaces and say 'Wishing Star Palace.'"

Charlotte and Mia exchanged curious looks. Normally, after granting a wish, they went home. They quickly pulled out their pendants. "Wishing Star Palace!" they cried together.

The surface of the pond started to swirl with light and sparkles spiralled into the air.

"Here we go!" gasped Charlotte, grabbing Mia's hand as the light surrounded them and whisked them away.

CHAPTER ELEVEN
Back at the Palace

The girls tumbled out of the tunnel of light on to the floor of the Mirror Room.

Princes Ella beamed with delight and helped them to their feet. "Welcome back!" she said, hugging them. "You were amazing. I'm so glad Tessa can take Baxter on holiday. She obviously loves him so much."

"She was really nice," said Charlotte.

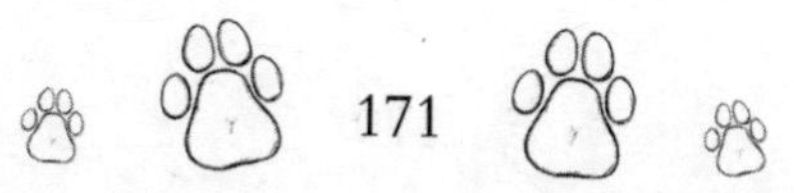

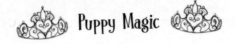

"I'm so glad we helped her."

"And Baxter was adorable," said Mia.

"You've earned your first rubies by granting her wish," said Princess Ella. "I really wish I could be the one to put them on your pendants, but unfortunately, without my wand, I can't. So let's go and find someone who can."

They followed her down the spiral staircase and then took a turning along a long corridor. At the end of the corridor were gold doors with a musical note sign.

"We haven't been here before," Charlotte said excitedly.

"The Music Room is one of Princess Alice's favourite places," said Princess Ella.

"She's been working on her new song all day but I bet she'll be delighted to know that you've granted another wish." She knocked on the door.

"Come in!" Alice called.

The Music Room was a large, airy room with big windows that looked out over the

palace grounds. Comfy chairs and sofas were scattered around the room, and against one wall there was a golden rack containing every musical instrument that you could possible imagine. Alice was curled up in one of the chairs with a guitar and a notebook. Her face lit up as she saw the girls.

“Hi!” she said. “What have you two been up to?”

“They’ve granted another wish!” said Ella. “And stopped Princess Poison from spoiling a wish with my wand.”

“Tell me all about it!” said Alice. “But first, let me get us all something to eat.

Granting wishes is hungry work!" She waved her wand and a wonderful afternoon tea appeared on a table. There was one cake stand filled with dainty sandwiches in the shape of musical notes and another piled with tiny cakes – little chocolate éclairs, bite-sized scones bursting with cream and jam, huge pink meringues and sugary doughnuts. There was sparkling lemonade or fruity tea to drink.

Charlotte's tummy rumbled. It felt like it had been a long time since they'd had an ice cream in the park!

"Help yourselves," said Alice, with a smile. "And then tell me what you did on your adventure this time."

As they all tucked into the delicious tea, Charlotte and Mia told Ella and Alice about Tessa and Baxter.

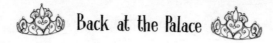

"You definitely earned your rubies today," Alice said as they finished. She picked up her wand. "Are you ready?"

They nodded eagerly and she touched her wand to each of their pendants.

There was a bright flash of red light and each half of the heart suddenly had a sparkling ruby embedded in it.

"Your first rubies," said Princess Ella, happily. "If you get three more, you'll pass

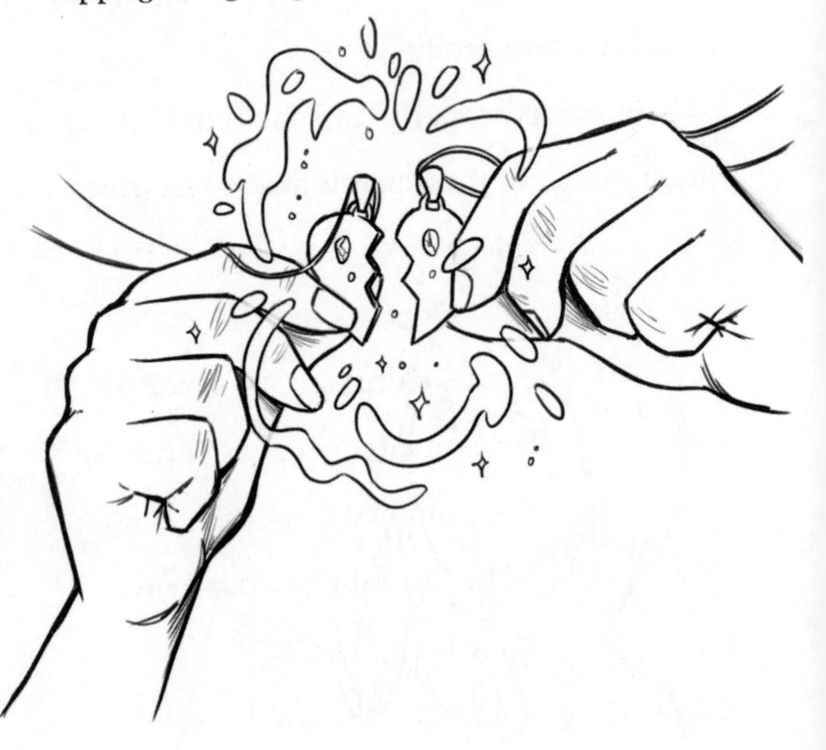

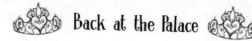

the second stage of princess training and get your magic princess slippers!"

"I can't wait until we grant another wish!" said Charlotte.

Mia nodded. "I love helping people with Charlotte." She smiled at her. "Actually, I love doing anything with Charlotte."

Alice gasped. "You know, that's just given me a great idea for the chorus of the song I'm working on. I've been struggling with a couple of lines, but I think I know what to say now." She strummed a couple of chords on the guitar and hummed to herself, then quickly wrote some notes in her notepad. "Yes, that's it!" she said in delight. "It's perfect. Do you want to hear it?"

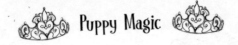

"Yes, please!" Mia and Charlotte said eagerly. Alice settled her guitar against her, strummed it, and then started to sing:

"*With friends the skies are always blue,*
And knowing them is a wish come true.
I can always count on my best friend,
She's by my side – from start to end!"

Mia and Charlotte held hands as Alice's sweet voice filled the room. It was incredible to think that they were the first people in the world to be hearing her new song. Soon, it would be playing on radio stations everywhere. Charlotte knew she'd remember this moment for the rest of her life.

As Alice finished, they all clapped loudly.

"Do you like it?" she asked hopefully.

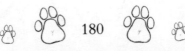

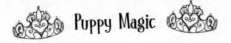

"I love it!" said Mia.

"It's a brilliant song," said Charlotte.

Ella nodded. "I bet it's going to be a huge hit." She sighed and got up. "This is so much fun, but I'm afraid I think it's time the girls went home."

Alice nodded.

Mia got to her feet and then remembered something. "What about the animals here?" she said. "We haven't got your wand back yet, Princess Ella. Does that mean the animals are still sad?"

"By granting Tessa's wish you broke that part of Princess Poison's curse," Ella said.

Alice waved her wand and conjured up two pairs of sparkling golden binoculars.

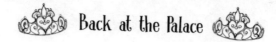

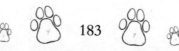

"If you look out of the window you'll be able to see for yourself." She handed the binoculars to the girls.

Peering through the binoculars out of the window, they could found they could see all the way across the Wishing Palace grounds to where the pond was. The flamingo-like birds' feathers were now bright neon colours again, the Rainbow Birds were strutting around showing off their magnificent tails, the unicorns were smiling happily and the

Tabbies were lounging on the grass, basking in the sunshine.

"They look really happy!" said Mia.

"They are," said Ella. "And it's all thanks to you two girls."

"Next time we'll try and get your wand back too," promised Charlotte.

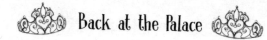

Princess Ella hugged her. "Thank you! I'm glad you're both training to be Secret Princesses."

Alice waved her wand and a tunnel of light appeared.

"Bye, Mia!" gasped Charlotte as she felt herself being pulled away. "See you soon!"

Charlotte slid down the shining tunnel of light and landed back in her bedroom. Hearing footsteps on the landing outside her room, she quickly jumped to her feet and smoothed her hair down.

"I'm just going to get lunch ready," said her mum, poking her head round Charlotte's bedroom door. "Do you want to come and help me?"

Charlotte nodded. Despite the afternoon tea she'd just eaten at Wishing Star Palace, she thought she could still manage some lunch. Alice was right – granting wishes really was hungry work!

"What do you fancy for lunch?" Charlotte's mum asked as they went downstairs.

Charlotte knew exactly what she wanted. "Hot dogs?" she suggested hopefully.

"Good idea," her mum said.

Charlotte linked her arm through her mum's. "That reminds me of a good joke! Why did the hot dogs turn down a chance to be in a film?"

"I don't know. Why?" said her mum.

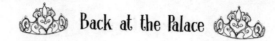

Charlotte grinned. "Because the roles weren't big enough. Get it? Roles, like rolls?"

Her mum chuckled. "Oh, Charlotte – you and your jokes. You'll have to tell Mia that one next time you talk to her on the computer."

Charlotte nodded, then grinned to herself.

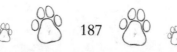

She couldn't wait to tell Mia the joke, but hopefully it wouldn't be on the computer – it would be when they next met at Wishing Star Palace!

The End

Join Charlotte and Mia in their next Secret Princesses adventure!

Read on for a sneak peek!

Prize Pony

"Does this look OK, Gran?" Mia held up the toy mouse she was making for her cat, Flossie. It was made out of white felt with a pink ribbon for a tail.

Her grandma put down her knitting. She was looking after Mia for the day. Mia loved it when it was just her and Gran because they always did fun craft projects.

"It's great," Gran said. "Now you just need the secret ingredient."

"What secret ingredient?" Mia asked curiously.

Gran took a plastic container out of her tapestry bag. "Catnip!" she said. "Cats love catnip."

Gran showed Mia how to use a funnel to fill the mouse with the dried herbs, and then Mia began the final bit of sewing. As she leant over with her needle, the golden pendant she was wearing fell forward. It was shaped like half a heart and it had a real ruby embedded in it. The ruby glittered in the sunlight streaming in through the window.

"Your necklace is very pretty," said Gran. "Is it new?"

"I've had it a few months now – I got it when Charlotte went to live in America," said Mia. "She has a matching one. We wear them all the time."

Gran smiled. "To help you remember each other? That's lovely."

"Mmm," said Mia, wondering what Gran would say if she told her the truth – that she didn't need a necklace to remember Charlotte, because she and Charlotte still saw each other all the time. Their necklaces were magic! Whenever their pendants started to glow, the girls were whisked away to an enchanted palace in the clouds.

Mia remembered how astonished she and Charlotte had been when they'd first visited Wishing Star Palace. It had been like having an amazing dream together

– particularly when they discovered that they had been chosen to train to be Secret Princesses. Secret Princesses could grant wishes to make people happy. They all lived in the real world, but they met up at Wishing Star Palace to have lots of magical, princessy fun. Every time Mia and Charlotte had visited the palace they had gone on an adventure and helped someone by using magic.

I really hope we go back to the palace soon, thought Mia as she cut the thread on her toy mouse. She jumped to her feet. "Here, kitty!" she called. "Flossie!"

Flossie came trotting through from the kitchen.

Kneeling down, Mia made the toy scurry along the ground like a real mouse. Flossie's green eyes widened and she pounced. Mia let go just in time as Flossie grabbed the mouse and started rolling over with it, batting it with her paws in delight.

Gran smiled. "A definite success! Cup of tea time, I think. Do you want a hot chocolate?"

"Yes please, Gran," said Mia.

Gran went into the kitchen, leaving Mia to carry on playing with Flossie. As Flossie rolled and pounced, Mia was reminded of Baxter, the bouncy puppy she and Charlotte had met on their last Secret Princess adventure. His owner, Tessa, had been very unhappy because she had thought he was going to fail his test at puppy-training school. Mia and Charlotte had helped her train Baxter and at the end of their adventure, a glittering ruby had appeared in each of their pendants. If they granted three more wishes and collected three more rubies, they would pass their second stage of training and get beautiful magic slippers to wear whenever they were at Wishing Star Palace.

A flash of light suddenly sparked across the surface of the pendant. Mia caught her breath as the whole pendant started to sparkle brightly. It was time for another magical adventure!

She glanced quickly at the door, but Gran was still in the kitchen making their drinks. Luckily, no time would pass at home while she was away on a Secret Princess adventure, so Gran wouldn't even notice that she was gone.

Mia wrapped her hand around the pendant and felt tingles running through her fingers. "I wish I could see Charlotte again," she whispered excitedly.

Light streamed out of the pendant and surrounded her in a sparkling whirlwind. Giving a squeal of delight, Mia felt herself being whisked away.

She twirled round and round like a ballerina until finally her feet landed on solid ground. The light cleared. Mia blinked, expecting to see the gardens of Wishing Star Palace, but she discovered she was standing in the middle of a sunny meadow at the foot of a hill. Scarlet poppies and golden buttercups danced in the breeze and pretty blue butterflies were swooping through the air. In the distance, Mia could see the pointed turrets of Wishing Star Palace reaching up into the blue sky.

Her forehead creased in confusion. Why was she so far away from the palace? Had the magic somehow gone wrong? She looked down and saw that she was wearing her golden princess dress and when she put her hand to her blonde hair, she felt her tiara nestling there.

"Mia!"

Charlotte appeared in the meadow in her rose-pink princess dress and a glittering diamond tiara. Her brown curls bounced on her shoulders and her hazel eyes sparkled with excitement. She raced towards Mia and swung her round in a tight hug. "Oh, it's so good to see you again!"

"And you! But where are we?" said Mia, hugging her back.

Charlotte looked round and Mia saw her frown as she realised they weren't in the gardens of the palace. "Weird. Do you think the magic's gone wrong?"

"That's what I was thinking," said Mia.

"I wonder where the princesses are."

Charlotte put her hands to her mouth and shouted. "Hello! Is anyone there?"

All they heard was the gentle rustling of the grass and flowers in reply.

Charlotte gave Mia a mystified look. "Maybe we should just start walking to the palace." She held out her hand. Mia was about to take it when they heard an echoey voice.

"Hellooooooo!"

They looked round.

"Hellooooooo!" The voice came again. "In heeeeeeeeere!"

"It's coming from inside the hill," said Charlotte in surprise. "Come on!

Let's go and investigate!"

"Wait!" Mia grabbed her. "What if it's Princess Poison?"

Princess Poison was a Secret Princess who had turned bad and used her magic to ruin people's wishes. Every time she managed to make someone unhappy, she became more powerful. So far, she had turned up on every one of Charlotte and Mia's adventures – but, by working together, they had always managed to beat her!

"Come and seeeeeeeeeee!" said the voice.

Charlotte frowned. "It can't be Princess Poison becasue she's been banished from Wishing Star Palace. Let's try and find whoever it is."

Holding hands, they walked cautiously towards the hill.

"In heeeeeeeeeeeeeere!"

Charlotte pointed to a dark opening in the base of the hill. "There's a cave! The voice is coming from in there!"

Heart pounding, Mia followed her best friend to the cave entrance. It looked dark and gloomy. Whatever were they going to find inside?

Read *Prize Pony* to find out what happens next!

Charlotte's Top Dog Jokes

What do you get if you cross a dog and a telephone?

A golden receiver!

What's a dog's favourite type of pizza?

Pupperoni!

Why did the dog say "moo"?

It was learning a new language!

What type of dog does a vampire have?

A bloodhound!

What kind of dog likes taking a bath?

A shampoodle!

What type of dog does a vampire have?

A bloodhound!

What's a dog's favourite hobby?

Collecting fleas!

Princess Ella's Puppy Care Tips

Playful puppies are lots of fun – but they are also a big responsibility! Are you up to the job? Here, Princess Ella tells you what it takes to look after a puppy.

- Always make sure your puppy has plenty of clean water to drink.

- Ask your vet what to feed your puppy. A growing dog needs healthy food to keep it fit and its coat and teeth in good condition.

- When it's old enough to go outside, give your puppy plenty of exercise by taking it for walks. It's good for you, too!

- Take your puppy to the vet for regular check-ups. Puppies need injections to stay healthy and stop them from getting ill. They also need protection against fleas and worms, which can give them itchy skin and an upset tummy.

Equipment List:

- Food and water bowls
- Bed
- Collar and lead
- Brush and comb
- Poop scoop and plastic bags
- Chew Toys

Dos and Don'ts

DO make sure your puppy always wears a collar with an identification tag. It is also a good idea to get your puppy micro-chipped in case it gets lost.

DON'T take a puppy away from its mother until it is at least eight weeks old.

DO remove anything you don't want your puppy to chew – as well as anything that could be poisonous.

DON'T feed your puppy scraps from the table. It could upset its tummy!

♥ WIN A PRINCESS GOODY BAG ♥

Secret
PRINCESSES
What would you wish for?

Design your own dress and win a Secret Princesses goody bag for you and your best friend!

Charlotte and Mia get to wear beautiful dresses at Wishing Star Palace, but now they want you to design one for them.

To enter all you have to do is follow these steps:

Go to **www.secretprincessesbooks.co.uk**

- Click the competition module
- Download and print the activity sheet
- Design a beautiful dress for Charlotte or Mia
- Send your entry to:

Secret Princesses: Ruby Collection Competition
Hachette Children's Group
Carmelite House
50 Victoria Embankment
London
EC4Y 0DZ

Closing date: 31st March 2017
For full terms and conditions,
visit www.hachettechildrens.co.uk/terms

Good luck!